tuned in

EPISODE #7

surprise
sleepover

by Julia DeVillers

introduction

This Journal Belongs to: ☆

☆ Maddy Elizabeth Sparks ☆

Private! Keep Out!!!

Q: What's my fave sport???!

A: Cheerleading!

Q: What's my fave food???!

A: Pizza!

OK! So I'm all in a happy mood here. Because I'm at the after school Cheerleaders Pizza Party!

I'm gonna share a pizza with Danielle, Shana and Chelsea B. Yum! I'm holding our table.

We just had cheerleading practice. I did pretty good! I didn't screw up the words to the new cheer! I didn't fall off the pyramid! I didn't bruise, twist or hurt myself today!

OK g2g ... Amanda is telling me something ...

OK I'm back! We're gonna have a cheerleader car wash. I'll be there! Oh yeah! Count me in! On all things cheerleady!

Before, when I didn't make cheerleading? Well, I felt all left out. You know.

But now? Not left out anymore! Yay!

g2g! Pizza's here!

chapter 1

"Skooch over, Maddy," Danielle said. Chelsea B sat across from us. Next to the pom-poms and book bag stuff.

"Half pepperoni and half veggie!" Chelsea B said.

We all started eating. Yum! Cheesy! Whoa. Really cheesy. And drippy. And messy.

"I'm going to get some more napkins," I said. I got up and went over to the napkin thingy. I waved at some other cheerleaders at another booth. Hi Quinn! Hi Amanda!

Brittany, Haley and Jada were sitting in another booth. I wasn't listening on purpose. Seriously! I was just pulling napkins out of the napkin thingy. But this is what I heard.

"Remember when Haley got stuck in her sleeping bag?!" Brittany was saying.

"Oh, that was so funny," Jada said. "She was all, help me! I can't get out!"

They were cracking up.

That would've been pretty funny. I thought about the sleepovers we'd been to. But I didn't remember Haley getting stuck.

"That was way fun," Jada was saying. "I was so tired yesterday."

Yesterday? Was there a sleepover this weekend?

"Danielle even fell asleep in math this morning," Brittany said.

Danielle was there, too?

Oooo-K! So. There was a sleepover this weekend.

NOT on the invite list? ME.

"Brittany, your slippers were the cutest!" I heard Haley squeal.

"Thanks," Brittany said. "Remember those slippers Maddy wore that one time? Those huge frog ones with the googly eyes? Totally shame-worthy. I was all, 'Nice slippers, Maddy.'"

"And she thought you were serious and was all like, 'Thanks!'" Haley said.

They all were cracking up again.

Oh. I thought my frog slippers were cute. OK, they were the biggest slippers I ever saw in my life. And bright green. And googly. But cute! I thought, at least. I thought Brittany thought so, too.

So. OK. Well.

I had like 200 napkins by now. I went back over to my booth. Danielle, Shana and Chelsea B were still eating pizza.

"Hey," I said. "Um, did you guys hear anything about a sleepover this weekend?" I asked. Like doo doo doo, no big deal.

"Nope," Chelsea B said. All cheerful.

"Danielle?"

"Um," Danielle said.

"Brittany kinda had a slumber party thing this weekend," Shana mumbled.

Oh. I looked at Danielle.

"A secret sleepover?" I asked.

"I didn't want to say anything," Danielle said. "I mean, I didn't want to make you guys feel bad."

"That's OK," Chelsea B said. "It's not like Brittany ever invited me anywhere anyway."

Yeah. Brittany didn't talk to Chelsea B. They kinda had a fight. Way back in second grade. Brittany holds a major grudge.

But Brittany always invited me to sleepover parties. Before, anyway.

"I hope you're not mad," Shana said. "Just because all the other cheerleaders were invited."

Oh.

"I didn't know you weren't invited til we got there," Danielle said. "It wasn't that fun anyway. All Brittany wanted to do was prank call guys."

"Yeah," Shana said. "Like when she called Ryan Moore three times and then his mother was like who is this and everyone was like laughing and –"

This got worse and worse. I shlumped in my seat.

"Maddy," Quinn called from another table. "Your Mom's here!"

Good timing! Thanks, Mom.

"Gotta go," I said. "See ya."

UCH! BLUCH!

OK, so. Brittany and I weren't officially friends anymore. But being left out of a sleepover? Way not fun.

And Brittany calling my slippers stupid? Everyone laughing?

Blugh.

"Bye, Maddy!" Brittany said.

I heard Brittany saying to my Mom, "Hiiiii, Mrs. Sparks. I like your hair."

"Thank you, Brittany. How nice of you to notice," my Mom said.

Blugh and Blugh.

"How was your day, Maddy?" my Mom asked when we got in the car.

"I so do not want to talk about it right now, OK?" I said.

My Mom looked at me.

"Sorry. I'm just in a way bad mood," I said.

"Let me know if you want to talk," Mom said. She turned on the radio.

I wonder how late they stayed up. I wonder what they talked

about. I wonder if they all did manicures like at the last sleepover Brittany had.

That I had been invited to.

I needed to think of something else. I opened my backpack.

- ☆ Lip gloss #1: Mango
- ☆ Lip gloss #2: Bubble gum
- ☆ Two gel pens: Blue glitter and black regular
- ☆ A book (but I'd finished it and needed a new one)
- ☆ My diary

I could fill out my diary! I had a new diary. It was different from my journal where I write down everything. The diary had questions to answer. I opened it.

Name: Maddy Elizabeth Sparks

My sign is: Libra!

For people who don't know me I would describe myself as: (Hm, this is hard. Um ...) Nice, a good friend, dog lover!

True or False:

I would rather live in a big city than a small town. T
I prefer the snow over the sand. F (winter is fun! But I looove the beach!)
I am more of a leader than a follower. F (F for follower.

Except sometimes, like at the dog shelter, I guess I can be a leader!)

I am more likely to be wearing tennis shoes than trendy heels. Kinda T, kinda F.

Rate the following from 1-10 (1 being 'I will only do if I have to' and 10 being 'one of my most fave things to do'):

> **Going to the movies –** 10
> **Camping –** 7
> **Cleaning my room –** 1
> **Shopping –** 10
> **Painting my nails –** 8
> **Playing sports –** 8
> **Dancing –** 8
> **Talking on the phone –** 9
> **Surfing the web –** 9
> **Slumber parties –**

OK ... see, I usually rate slumber parties a 10!!

Except when I'm not invited to them! Then I rate them a ... big fat **ZERO!!!**

Our car pulled in the driveway. I shut my diary. I needed some cheering up. And I knew what would cheer me up!!!

chapter 2

I opened the front door. I made kissy noises ... mwah! Mwah!

I heard little tiny footsteps coming down the hall and there was ...

BUGGIE!

My cute little Lovebug puppy!

Buggie was so happy to see me too! I petted her fluffy white fur. She licked my face with her little pink tongue! She was all squirmy, like, Maddy's home! Yay!!!

I am so happy I have a dog!

Did I always have a dog?

Nope, no way.

But then Dad finally said ...

YES!!!

And now, I have my cutest little sweetest Buggie!!!!!!

I carried Buggie upstairs to my room. I plopped her on my bed.

Then I heard, Prrrp! Prrrp!

"Be right back," I kissed Buggie's nose. I got up and went over to my guinea pig's cage.

"Don't worry Sugar," I said. "I still love you." I picked up Sugar and brought her over to the bed. I lay down, with Buggie on one side. Sugar on the other. I picked up my journal again.

OK! Feeling better now! I have Buggie! I have Sugar!

But then I heard this noise. Under my bed.

ZWAK! ZWAK!

And WHOMP! This big thing jumped on my bed!

Ack! Buggie bounced into the air! Sugar bounced into the air! Sugar started kicking her legs and making that guinea pig noise, SQUEE!!!!

It was Rex!

Yes, Rex! My brother's new dog! Not just any dog. Rex was round and brown with wrinkles. He had chubby short little legs. And one tooth sticking out like a fang. Part Bulldog, Part ... I'm not sure.

Rex turned around and round. Then snuggled himself in my

sheets.

OK, I mean, I like dogs. I looooove dogs. But my brother's Dog? He was ... um ... hard to live with. He did things like ...

AH-SNEEZE!

Like sneeze! Which made greenish goo all over my pillow. Ewww, OK, this was just sick!!!

Ack! I grabbed Sugar! I grabbed Buggie! And jumped off the bed before we were gooey, too!

See this is why Rex is a good name for him. He WRECKS everything!!!

"ZACK!" I yelled.

I heard footsteps. Zack ran in.

"Hey, what's my dog doing in here?" Zack said. "You have your own dog! Don't try to steal mine."

Steal him?

"No way!" I yelled. "Your dog just busted in here. He freaked out Sugar. And then he goo-ed all over my bed!" I tried to push Rex off. He snuggled into my pillow.

Snortle! Snortle! Rex made some of his seriously weird noises. Then he wiggled and jiggled. Then he chased his tail.

OK, I had to admit. Rex was kinda funny!

"I'll get him," Zack said.

He tried to pick up Rex. But Rex was heavy! And squirmy! Zack went whooooaaa ... and kaboomp!

They both landed on the floor. Rex started licking Zack's face.

"Yipes!" said Zack. "Your breath is stinkus!"

Buggie looked at me. I looked at Buggie. I was smiling. I think she thought it was kinda funny, too!

Zack finally got Rex out of my room.

Whew.

"Rex, stay out of girl territory," I heard Zack say. "You'll get girl germs. Gross."

Oh puh-lease.

I yanked off my gooey pillowcase! Into the laundry. Then I lay back on my bed and got all comfy again. Left side: Buggie. Right side: Sugar.

Ah, totally relaxing. Me, my dog, my guinea pig. Just us.

Snortle! Snortle! Snuff! I heard a breath under my door. Oh no. It was back.

Scratch, scratch. Scratch, scratch. That dog was trying to break in to my room! This dog was just like my brother! Zack always tried to bust in my room, too!

AUGH!!!

"Zack!" I yelled. "Your dog!"

I heard Zack's footsteps. I heard Zack struggle to drag Rex away.

Buh-bye. Now. Back to relaxing.

"Maddy!" I heard my Mom yell. "Did you clean your room?"

AUGH!

I'd rated cleaning my room a 1! As in I HATE to clean my room. Did I have to do that NOW?

I wish my Mom was calling up for me to do something I'd rank a 10! Or a 9! Even a 6!

I got up off my bed. I started to clean. Clean, clean, cleaning my room. Blah blah boring boring. Stuff on floor ... picked up. Bed ... made.

I looked around my room. I love my room! It's blue! My fave color. I have a blue comforter with this white net coming down over my bed. I have my shell collection and lots of pictures of my friends. I have made my closet door into a collage-thing of posters from magazines. Guys on my Ultimate Crush List!

My posters were these guys:

> ★ The guys in that new band who sing that new song? Sooo hot! They're my #4, 5, and 6 crushes!!!
> ★ Austin Hamilton! The TV star! My #3 crush! I even met him once in California! I'm serious!
> ★ Carter McLain! The movie star! My new #2 crush! And he's going to be in a new movie playing a prince! I can't wait to see it!

Oh. I don't have a picture of #1 on my Ultimate Crush List. No way. Too secret! Because he's not on TV or a singer or in the movies ... it's Ryan Moore.

Yup. Ryan Moore!

In my school!

Dark brown hair. Deep blue eyes. Way cute.

Werf! Buggie made a little bark. She was looking up at me with her huge eyes.

"Doesn't our room look nice?" I asked her.

Buggie just looked at me. I looked around. Was she trying to tell me something? Ohhhhh. It's Buggie's room, too! Sugar has her cage. But Buggie didn't have anything of her own.

"Buggie, you need a spot for you, right?"

Buggie said werf! I think she meant yes!

"Princess Lovebug," I told her, "We'll make you a space perfect for a princess." I moved some stuff out of a corner of my room.

I got out a little pillow. One that Rex hadn't slimied up! I put it in one of the corners of my room. I put her fave pink and white blanket on the pillow. I put a little beany puppy on it for her to snuggle with.

"Tada!" I told her. "You have a throne."

I got out some paper, markers and glittery glue. I made a sign.

I stuck the sign to the wall with sticky stuff.

"OK, Buggie," I said. "You can look now!" I carried her over. I put her on the pillow. She snuggled into the pillow and went SIGH.

"I think you like it!" I said. "That is your special sleeping space."

And then ... I heard this noise.

ZWAK! ZWAK!

The door busted open!

It was Rex!

chapter 3

Rex pushed my door right open! Before I could stop him, he raced over to Buggie's new space. He jumped on it! Buggie jumped off! Rex started kicking his legs around! The blanket flew off! The beany dog flew off!

"Rex!" I screamed. "Stop wrecking Buggie's space! Out!" I tried to push him off. He wasn't moving.

"Zack!" I yelled. "Get your beast out of my room!"

Then Rex got up, went into my closet, and came out carrying ... my frog slipper.

He was chewing on one of my frog slippers.

"Hey! That's mine!" I said. I started to grab it. But wait. I remembered they were stupid. I thought about Brittany. Totally making fun of them.

"Go ahead, Rex," I said. "Chew away. Chew that into teeny, tiny pieces."

Then Zack bursted in. He looked at Rex.

"Rex!" he said. "Yeesh! What are you thinking, dude! Come on.

We got guy stuff to do." Zack looked at me. "Can't you lock your door or something? Yeesh."

Then he tugged on Rex's collar and dragged him away.

OK, augh!

That dog is seriously making me cra-zay!!!

"Sorry, Buggie," I said. "I'll fix your bed." I threw my slippers to the back of the closet. I fluffed up her pillow. I put back her blanket. I set her on her bed. Then I got out a marker. And added to the sign.

Princess Lovebug's Space

No Rex Allowed! Keep out!

I was done cleaning! Kewl! Now I could do something fun! Something I wouldn't rate a "1" in my diary. Something like ...

Dling!

E-mailing! My computer made a noise that I had a new e-mail. Kewl! E-mailing my friends rated a 10! I love e-mail! I ran over to my computer.

```
From: BrittanyCheer
Send to: Haleygrl
Cc:  Amandapanda,  Dani55,  Shanastar,  Jadarox,
ChelCB, CareBear143, QuinnQT, Maddyblue
Subject: Cheerleader Car Wash!

It's your Cheerleading captain! The cheerleader car
wash is Saturday at 10 am!

Don't 4get. Caroline and Jada r in charge of supplies!

Maddy ur in charge of publicity. I haven't seen
any??? R U slacking?

Xoxox Brittany
```

OK, huh? I'm in charge of what??? I'm slacking on what???
This was way news to me.

I IM'd Brittany.

```
MaddyBlue: I didn't know I was in charge of publicity?

BrittanyCheer: I sent you an e-mail to tell u. u
need to make posters and make sure EVERY1 knows!!

MaddyBlue: I do?

BrittanyCheer: If no1 shows up every1 will blame
u. g2g. my private cheer tutor is coming.

* BrittanyCheer signed off *
```

AUGH!

I bet she never realllly sent me that e-mail.

Because Brittany and I were ... not getting along! We had to sit next to each other on the bus. We had to cheerlead together. But we were so not talking to each other unless we had to.

OK. Pressure!

I looked at the sign I'd made for Princess Buggie. I got my markers back out.

"Buggie, it looks like I'll be making a lot more signs tonight!" I sighed. Great. I had to let people know about the car wash. If people didn't show up, Brittany would blame me!

Write write write write. CAR WASH SATURDAY! CAR WASH SATURDAY! CAR WASH SATURDAY! CAR WASH SATURDAY! CAR WASH SATURDAY! CAR WASH SATURDAY!

I wrote my gajillionth sign. My hand was tired! Exhausted! About to fall off!

I'd cleaned my room! I'd made signs! It was time to relax! And get comfy. I got out some pajamas and put them on. They were pink with cute little doggies wearing princess crowns. I put on my fluffy matching pink robe. Ah ... time to rest and relax. Do something fun!

Then the phone rang.

"Maddy!" my Mom yelled. "It's for you!"

Cool. I'd rated "talking on the phone" a 9 in my diary! I looove to be on the phone! Unless it was Brittany of course. Calling to remind me that I had to, like, bake a billion brownies for a cheerleader bake sale tomorrow. Or something I knew nothing about. I would rate that a NEGATIVE 9.

I got the phone.

"Hi Maddy, it's Lauren." Lauren! From Limited Too! Yay! Whenever she called, something exciting was going to happen!

"Hi Lauren!" I said into the phone.

"I have your next assignment for you," Lauren said. "Do you like sleepovers?"

OK, we know the answer to that one!

Yes, yes, and yes!

"I love sleepovers!" I told Lauren.

"Great," she said. "Because you're going to be hosting one. A big one. With the TOO Crew of course. We'll all meet at Headquarters tomorrow to do some planning."

Cool!

This time I got to put on the sleepover! I'd had a couple sleepovers at my house. Small ones. Like when my BFF Taylor slept over. We stayed up til 2 in the morning and ate about 10 bowls of popcorn. And once Taylor and Danielle and Brittany and Haley slept over for my birthday. We watched this scary movie and freaked ourselves out

What are we were going to do at THIS sleepover?? I can't wait to find out!

chapter 4

I entered the Limited Too headquarters. It's this big white building with lots of windows. I got buzzed in.

"Hi, Maddy!" the woman at the front desk said. She knows my name. How cool is that?! She gave me a visitor's badge on a rope thingy. I hung it around my neck like a necklace.

"Hi Maddy!" Lauren said. "The rest of the TOO Crew is here. Are you ready to plan a sleepover?"

"Yes!" I said. We went into a room and there was ...

Kacey! Isabel! Claire!

"MADDY!" Kacey, Isabel and Claire all said. All happy to see me! They were all sitting around a table. I sat in a chair next to Isabel. Lauren sat on the other side of me.

Lauren tuned us in on the whole sleepover deal. There would be a big sleepover with lots of girls IN THE MALL! After it closed!

The sleepover would be like a giant focus group. A focus group is where you give your opinions on things. So the people who make them can see what you think about them.

There would be different stations. Like, one station would be to test out lip glosses. Another one to see which candy tastes best. Then we would do some sleepover activities all together! So cool!

"And I'm hoping my reliable TOO Crew will help us think up activities," Lauren said. "And then help at the sleepover."

We were all like, Definitely!!!

So, we get to think of ideas for the sleepover. Lauren left us alone to come up with ideas.

"OK, what have you guys done at sleepovers?" Isabel asked. "Anyone been to a big one before?"

"Brittany had like 18 girls sleep over last year," I said. "Shana fell asleep first and Brittany drew mustaches on her face in marker. Then Brittany truth or dared Danielle to eat dog food and Danielle got all sick and –"

I stopped. OK, maybe Brittany's sleepover didn't have the best ideas.

"Here's what I think," Isabel said. "I think we need a theme. Something that ties it all together."

"How about sports?" Kacey said. "We could all wear uniforms and compete."

"Not bad," Isabel said. She wrote it down. "What else?"

"Horses?" Claire suggested. Claire's into horses. "Or I guess not. We can't really bring horses in or anything."

"Dogs," I said. Can you tell I like dogs? Isabel added it to the list.

"Fashion show?" Isabel said. We were like, yeah, that might be fun.

We all sat there thinking.

"What stations are there going to be again?" I asked. "Maybe that would give us ideas?"

"OK, here's a list Lauren left us!" Kacey said, jumping up to hand us all papers. That girl couldn't sit still in a seat for more than like a minute! We'd be doing stuff like test new lip glosses, candy, songs for a movie soundtrack ...

"Oh wow," I said, reading the details. "We get to rate songs for that new movie. The one where Carter McLain plays a prince!"

We all went ... AHHHHH. Because Carter McLain? Way cute.

"Carter McLain is the perfect Prince Charming," Claire sighed.

"How about a princess theme?" I suggested.

Isabel looked up. "That's not a bad idea!"

"Do you think that would be kinda babyish?" Kacey worried.

"Not really," Claire said. "I mean, I liked princess stuff when I was little but I still like it now, too!"

"Oh, yeah me too!" Kacey said. "I mean I totally love princess-like movies. And imagine if you lived in a castle and ...."

We were cracking up! Kacey is very talky!

"This could be a winner!" Isabel said. "Especially since we're voting on that movie music. We could play the music."

"How about having makeovers so we're princesses?" I said.

"Definitely," Isabel said, writing it down.

"We could decorate like a castle," Claire suggested.

"Oo ya! And we could say everyone is being treated like a princess!" Kacey said, all bouncy and excited.

"Who votes for the princess theme?" Isabel said.

Everyone was all, Me! Me! Me! And Me!

"That was a great idea, Maddy," Claire said.

Aw! Yay! We started writing down more ideas. Like things to do. Ways to decorate. All kinds of stuff. Way exciting. Way glam! This sleepover was going to be ... FUN!!!!!

Lauren came back in. We told her all of our ideas.

"I'm impressed," she said. "And, this theme gives me a few more ideas. We're doing some tie-ins with that movie we're testing the soundtrack for."

"The one with Carter McLain?" I asked.

"Yes," Lauren said. "I'll talk to the movie people about some ideas when they come to town this week."

We were all, ooooh, movie people!

"You've come up with some good ideas," Lauren said. "But I want you girls to have fun too. So I'll keep a few surprises for the sleepover up my sleeve."

I CAN'T WAIT!

"For now, let's take a break," Lauren said. "Ice cream anyone?"

We all walked into the company cafeteria. There were a few ice cream choices!

"Yay! They have my fave, cookie dough," Kacey said, dancing around.

Isabel got vanilla. Claire got rainbow sherbet.

Maddy's List of Fave Ice Cream Flavors:

- ★ Mint chocolate chip
- ★ Cookies and cream
- ★ Rocky road
- ★ Chocolate

I got mint chocolate chip. We went and sat at a table.

We were all talking about everything! Claire was like riding horses-playing violin-new friend Hannah. Isabel was like fashion-sketching class-cheerleading. Kacey was like lacrosse-soccer-basketball.

I was like volunteering at pet shelter-Buggie-cheerleading.

"Speaking of cheerleading, how's Brittany treating you?" Isabel asked.

Isabel sorta tries to help me with Brittany. Because, well, I need help dealing with that girl! Well ... actually ...

"The whole sleepover thing?" I said. "At least I get to go to THIS one. Brittany had one. I didn't get invited."

"Well, that's probably good!" Kacey said. "Since she's not been nice to you!"

"Yeah, I guess," I said. "Except everyone else went. And then my other friends were like, 'Oh yeah. We wanted to keep it a secret from you!'"

"That's hard," Claire said.

"Anyway," I said. "Enough about me. Kacey! Any baby?"

"Any day!" Kacey said. "Any minute!"

Kacey's Mom is pregnant. She's going to have a little sister. Or brother! They don't know.

"Have you picked out names yet?" Claire asked. Kacey gets to pick out the name!!!

"Not yet!" Kacey said. "I can't decide! It's all so confusing!"

And then something weird happened. Kacey actually looked ... SAD. Not her usual happy self. She wasn't bouncing around all happy! She was sitting there looking ... well, bummed out.

"Kacey, um, is something wrong?" I asked her.

"Oh, well," Kacey said. "I was just, well, I mean I'm really excited about the baby. Really. I love my little sister Emily. But maybe it sounds stupid ... it's just everything's going to change in my house! And now I have to share a room with Emily! And she makes these noises when she sleeps. Like khhh khhh," Kacey was talking all fast.

Poor Kacey. I mean, it's exciting! But I could see her being all nervous, too. Especially if the baby is a brother. A brother like Zack. That would make anyone cccccrrrrraaaaazzzzzy!!!!!!

"It's going to be hard," Isabel said. "But I still think you're lucky. I mean, Jessica and Michael are great. But it would be nice to have someone to look up to me in the house!"

"And I think you're so lucky," Claire said. "I don't have any brothers or sisters in my house!"

They all looked at me.

"Well," I said. "I survive Zack. OK, he is kinda funny. And even nice. Sometimes. But don't tell him I said so."

"And if you need to escape Emily's snoring?" Claire said. "Come sleep over at my house. I mean, the more sleepovers the better, right?! Like our Princess Pajama Party!"

"I know," I said. "We'll have a celebration for you when the baby's born. OK?"

"Yeah, great idea," Isabel said. "So plan on celebrating with us! Big sister style"

"I will!" Kacey said. And yay! She was all smiley again!!!

chapter 5

Cheerleader Car Wash TODAY!

"C-A-R! The cheerleaders are who we are!"

Brittany was calling out cheers. I heard her as we pulled into the parking lot. A bunch of cheerleaders were running around. With sponges! Buckets! Hoses!

My first cheerleader's car wash! As a cheerleader!

"W-A-S-H—Um ...hey!" Brittany stopped. "What rhymes with H?"

"Great?" Danielle suggested. "This car wash is really great?"

"That doesn't rhyme!" Brittany snapped.

I climbed out of my car. I had Buggie with me!

"Zack and I will take Buggie for a walk while we wait," Dad said.

Oh. I also had Zack with me, too.

SNOOOORE, SNOOOORE.

We also had Rex with us. He was sleeping. In the back seat.

And snoring.

"We'll leave Rex here," Dad said.

Good.

"Hi Maddy!" everyone said. And then they went ...

Awwwwww! Because they saw Buggie! I walked Buggie over to everyone.

"She's sooooooo cute!" Chelsea B said.

Everyone was petting Buggie. Even Brittany was like, ohhhh! So cute!

"I should have brought my dog, Angel!" Quinn said. "They could have had a puppy playdate!"

"I brought MY dog, too!" someone said.

It was Zack. He came over and was all butting in.

"You should see MY dog," he said. "He's way cooler."

"This is my brother Zack," I said in case anyone didn't know. "He's SUPPOSED to stay out of our way!"

"Excuuuse me," Zack said. "Dad told me to come take Buggie."

"Awwww. He's soooo cute!" Amanda said.

"Buggie's a girl," I told her.

"No, I mean your little brother," Amanda said. "He's just so adorable!"

"Adorable?" Zack said, backing away.

"He's such a little sweetie!" Jada agreed. She patted Zack's head.

"Sweetie? Yipes! Too many girls," Zack said. "Give me your dog, Maddy! Quick!"

I kissed Buggie's nose. I gave her to Zack and he took off.

"Bye Buggie! I'll miss you! Bye Zack! I'll miss you ... NOT!"

"Girls!" Brittany announced. "Where were we before Maddy interrupted everything?"

Yeesh.

"Trying to find a word that rhymes with H?" Haley said.

"OK, whatever on that! The cars will be coming soon! Places everyone!" Brittany screamed.

We all ran to our places.

I checked my schedule.

First: Hold up signs at street.

Second: Wash cars.

OK! I went over to the street. It was me, Danielle, Quinn and Chelsea B.

"These are great signs," Quinn said.

"Thanks!" I told her. I worked hard on those things!

Brittany came over.

"Your job is to get the cars in," Brittany said. "Maddy, I hope your signs are big enough. Otherwise nobody will see them and then we won't raise any money and this whole thing will be a total disaster."

Oooo-K! I didn't say anything.

"I'm going to do a last-minute sponge check," Brittany said. "OK, it's time. Hold up those signs, cheerleaders."

We all held up our signs.

We were all screaming at cars. Waving our hands! Pointing at the cars!

I hope my signs are big enough.

And then, a car pulled in! We waved it to the car wash. And then another one!

Car wash! Car wash!

A lot of cars were pulling in!

"This is great!" said Quinn. "We're going to raise a lot of money!"

A white SUV pulled up near us. The window rolled down and some heads stuck out of it.

"Hey, it's some basketball players!" said Chelsea B. "Hi Brandon! Hi Ryan!"

Ryan! Ryan Moore? Yes! That Ryan Moore!

Some hands waved out of the car. Ryan's mother was driving.

"Hi Mrs. Moore!" Quinn said. Quinn lives near Ryan Moore.

Lucky.

"Hello, girls!" Mrs. Moore said through the window. "Hello, Quinn. And who might you girls be?"

"I'm Chelsea B. That's Danielle and Maddy," Chelsea B said.

Danielle goes "Hi!"

And I go, "GAH!"

Yes, GAH!

OK, OK, I know. But it's RYAN MOORE'S MOTHER!!!

"Nice to meet you girls," she said. "Maddy, I've heard about you."

RYAN MOORE TOLD HIS MOTHER ABOUT ME!!!

"Ma!" Ryan said.

"Well, I guess we should get in line," Ryan's mother said. "Where do I go for the car wash?"

We all pointed at the line. They drove away.

OK, wait. RYAN MOORE TOLD HIS MOTHER ABOUT ME!!!

I wonder what he said.

"Attention all Cheerleaders!" Brittany yelled. "It's time to switch! Please move to your next station."

"Time to wash cars!" Danielle said.

Time to stop thinking about what Ryan Moore told his mother about me! We went over and got sponges. And buckets of soapy water. And hoses.

"Let's go that way," I pointed at a green minivan.

Because it wasn't a white SUV with Ryan Moore and his mother in it! I didn't want to be like GAH again.

And besides. Brittany was already over at the car with the basketball players.

"Brittany," Amanda was calling out. "Aren't you supposed to be holding signs?"

Washing car time! Me and Danielle sponged and soaped the front of the van. Chelsea B and Quinn sponged and soaped the back. Scrubbing! Scrubbing!

The van looked great! Shiny and sparkly. And then a new car pulled into the parking lot. And it made everyone go ...

"OH!"

Because it was a limo! A huge long black limo.

chapter 6

"Wow! Nice wheels," I heard someone say.

"OK! OK!" Brittany came running back. "I think this needs my supervision!" Haley followed her.

"Yah, right," Danielle said. "They just want to see who's in that limo."

And then the limo pulled over to us.

"Hello," a guy with a cap rolled down the window. "Can you tell me how to get to Oak Street?"

"Absolutely," Brittany said. She was trying to peek in the back. You could so tell! But the windows were dark.

"First though, wouldn't you like to support the Tigers?" Brittany said. "It's a cheerleader car wash."

"I'm sorry, I would," the limo driver told her. "But we have to be somewhere on schedule."

"Take a left there and go that way," she said. Brittany leaned in. She peeked in the back. And went, "OH!" And jumped back.

The limo guy thanked her and started to drive away. Brittany says, "Oh. My. Gosh. I saw who was in the back of that limo. I am so serious. I think it was CARTER MCLAIN!!!!"

Really?

"Nuh uh," said Haley. "No WAY!"

"That could be true," Chelsea B said. "My Mom said they were doing some stuff here in town this week. For a movie premiere."

"And how does your Mom know that?" Brittany asked.

"She does a lot of the events in town," Chelsea B told her. "So she knows these things."

Brittany looked at Chelsea B like, Hm. Interesting.

"Ohmigosh," Danielle said. "So you really saw Carter McLain! What did he look like? What did he do?!!"

"Well," Brittany said. "He had on a baseball hat. And he uh, waved to me! And he uh, winked, too! Yes! That's right! Can you guys believe it! Carter McLain winked at me!"

"Maybe he likes you!" Haley said.

Brittany just shrugged all like, maybe true!

"You guys!" Haley screamed out. "Everybody! Carter McLain was in that limo! And he likes Brittany!"

All the cheerleaders rushed over for scoop.

"Yeah, right," Danielle whispered to me. "Can Brittany get any more attention or what?"

Really. But still. Was that really Carter McLain in that limo? Ohmigosh. Did we really get THIS close to Carter McLain? How cool would that be?

"Carter McLain is so cute!" I said. This was some car wash! Carter McLain (even if I didn't see him)! Ryan Moore (even if I said GAH to his Mom)!!

But it was back to car washing!

We washed cars! SUVs! Minivans! Danielle and Quinn and I were hard at work! Chelsea B was trying to be. But Brittany kept asking her questions.

"So your Mom works with a lot of stars?" Brittany asked Chelsea B.

"Kind of, if there's an event in town or something," Chelsea B told Brittany.

"I didn't know that," Brittany said. "Do you ever get tickets?

Do you ever get to bring people?"

Another car pulled up. It was an old white car.

"Yeah, like we'd ever get that car clean," Brittany said. All snotty.

It did have rust and spots and was kinda beat up.

"Hi," I went over. "Do you want a car wash?"

"Sure!" a lady said. "We're here in town for an event. And the girls saw your sign!"

Four girls got out of the car.

"We just did a car wash last weekend! We raised money to help clean up a park in our neighborhood," one of the girls said.

"There's nowhere for the little kids to play," said another girl. "So we're trying to make a little playground."

"That's so nice," I said.

"I think getting our car washed would be nice," the lady said. "Since we want our girls to drive in style this weekend."

"Allison won a contest!" one of the girls said. "And she brought us!!!!"

The girls all went EEEEeeee! So excited!!!!

"Cool! Well, I'm Maddy," I said.

"We're Allison, Amber, Andi and Ami!" they said. "The four A's!"

These girls were way sweet! I hoped they had fun at their thing.

"You can wait over there, and then your car is up next."

Quinn, Chelsea B, Danielle and I started washing their car. We finished it and Chelsea B went to go tell them it was done.

Then I saw my Dad's car pull up!

"I'm here for the car wash," Dad said. He gave Danielle some money. Zack got out of the back. He was carrying Buggie.

"Oooh, let me hold her?" Quinn asked. She was holding Buggie. Buggie licked her. "Awww, she's soooo sweet!"

"Helloooo Mr. Sparks," Brittany said to my Dad all nicey nice. We all got sponges and got ready to wash my Dad's car. He went over to talk to some parents.

And then ...

ACKKKKKKKKKKKKK!

Brittany was screaming! Like ACKKKK! And pointing at my car.

And then I saw it.

Rex's face. Sticking out of the window.

He was all drooly.

"Oh, you woke Rex up," Zack said.

"What is that thing?!!!" Brittany screamed. "Some kind of freaky monster?!"

"Hey," said Zack. "That's very insulting."

And then Rex sneezed. WACHOO! One of his green, gooey sneezes! And it kinda um ... this is way gross ... got near Brittany.

Uh oh!

"Ewwww!" Brittany said.

"Here I'll get that off," Zack said. He got a sponge. And tried to wipe off Brittany's arm.

"Stop it! You're getting drippy all over me!" Brittany wailed.

"I'm just trying to help," Zack said.

"Just get away and take that stupid creature with you!" Brittany hissed at him. She and Haley started wiping her arm with paper towels.

"It was an accident, Zack," I said. Trying to make him feel all better.

"Yeah," Zack said. "Brittany didn't have to go all freaky. That girl is always mean to me."

He took Rex's leash and walked away.

I felt kinda bad for him. We washed the car.

"Do you really think that was Carter McLain in there?" I asked Danielle. "I wish we could have seen him!"

"I bet he didn't wink at Brittany, though," Danielle said. "She was all like, 'Oh yeah, and he winked at me.' I think she totally made that up."

"Want some help?" Zack came back over. My Dad was holding two leashes. Buggie and Rex.

"No, thanks," I said. "Cheerleaders only."

"I can be your mascot," he said.

No, nope, and no.

"I'm bored," he whined.

"Bye, Zack," I said. He wandered away. I washed and washed ...

And then I heard a scream. I looked over and saw ...

Zack ...

holding a hose ...

spraying a car!

Wait. It gets worse.

Because the water? Spraying over the top of the car. On the other side? Brittany!

"Whoops," Zack said all cheerful. "Didn't see you there."

Sure he didn't.

"Maddy!" Brittany yelled. "You can't let your brother crash the car wash! Look what he did! I am ALL WET!"

It wasn't MY fault! I told him no! ARGH!!!

And yup. Brittany was seriously wet. Very ... drippy. OK. It was kinda funny.

I looked at Danielle. "He has to pay," I said.

I took my pail of water. I snuck over to where Zack was spraying. And I ...

DUMPED THE BUCKET OVER ZACK'S HEAD!!!

"Gotcha!" I said. HA!

"Yipes!" he yelled.

Zack was soooo soaked. Totally wet!

And then Brittany took her sponge. And ohmigosh! She threw it at Zack!

And Zack sprayed the hose again! And hit me!

"Hey!" That was cold!

And then, I saw Brittany grab a hose. And she was spraying Zack! And then Haley did, too!

But then Zack was spraying everyone and ...

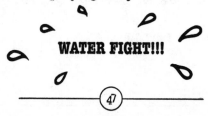

WATER FIGHT!!!

Hoses were spraying! Sponges were flying!

Everyone was like ... EEEEEEE!

"Hey!" I yelped! Danielle dumped a bucket of water over my head.

"I'll get you back!" I screamed. I sprayed her with my hose.

Our hair was dripping wet! Our clothes were dripping wet!

And we were ... CRACKING UP!

Even Brittany.

'Cuz it was crazy! And fun!

And then ...

"Girls!"

Uh.

Oh.

Brittany's Mom. She's our cheerleading coach.

And she didn't look too happy.

"What is going on here?"

Everyone was like, "Um ...."

"Maddy's little brother started it," Brittany said. "He sprayed me."

"Well, you called my dog freaky!" Zack said.

"I'm going to have a word with your father, young man," her Mom said. "And the rest of you clean up this mess."

We were all, yes, OK, uh huh.

I cleaned up my sponges. But when I looked at Danielle? She was still cracking up, too!

chapter 7

This Journal Belongs to: ☆

☆ Maddy Elizabeth Sparks
☆

Zack put this down! You're already in enough trouble!

I'm packing for the majorly huge sleepover! I made a list:

☆ Sleeping bag (sky blue)!

☆ My Build-A-Bear Workshop® Floppy Kitty named
    Pommy because she's wearing a cheerleading outfit.

☆ Toothbrush, toothpaste and stuff like that!

And of course ... my pajamas! We're wearing regular
clothes first. Then changing into PJs.

I'm packed! I'm ready! I'm PSYCHED!!!!!!!! G2g.

OK! So, this is so crazy! I mean, I shop here! Now I'm going to sleep here! I was feeling a little nervous. OK why? I mean, I am helping put this sleepover on, right? So I should be like la la la, I am helping host this party.

But I mean, I didn't know the girls coming! Besides the TOO Crew of course! So it felt a little weird. I saw a bunch of girls walking in. Carrying sleeping bags like me.

"Maddy, you can get out now," my Mom said. "Have fun, honey."

"Have fun, Stinky," Zack said. He was in the back seat with Rex.

I gave Buggie a kiss. "I'll miss you, little Lovebug," I told her. "Be a good puppy."

I opened the door. And was followed by ...

Rex! That dog wants to follow me everywhere! Augh!

"No, Rex," I said. "Get back in the car."

Rex looked at me and went:

SNORT! And then he started to waddle away.

Argh. I grabbed him by the collar. I tried to drag him back to the car. And then ...

DISASTER. Major serious disaster.

Rex, um ... had to go. I mean ... GO.

So he went.

And I was pulling on his leash and I um ... stepped in it!

Red-face Rating: ☆★★★☆ out of ☆★★★☆ stars.
So embarrassing and so totally sick. I can't even think about this.

"Oh nooooooo!" I screamed.

"Oh GROSS!" Zack said. He pretended to puke.

My shoes! My Mom came out to help me.

"Er, these are in pretty bad shape," my Mom said. "Let me put them in a bag."

I took them off.

P.U!

"Now I have no shoes!" I wailed. I looked at my outfit. I thought I looked kinda nice.

A light blue flowy shirt that I thought was kinda princess-y. A skirt.

My choker with a princess crown on it.

My TOO Crew charm bracelet.

And now ... bare feet?

"I can't let you go in bare feet," my Mom said. "It's a mall."

But oh no!

"Mom! I don't have time to go home!" I said. "I have to be in there! To help out!"

"Well, sweetie, I'm not sure what to tell you." Mom said.

"I can fix it!" Zack said. He stuck his head out the window. "Tada!"

And he was holding up ... my frog slippers. The ones Brittany was making fun of.

"Rex brought them in to chew on them," Zack said. "They're a little soggy. But not too much!"

"Um, thanks," I told him. But I can't wear those slippers! Not to this princess party! With my nice outfit?

Everyone would totally make fun of me!

But ... did I have a choice?

I took the slippers. I put them on.

I waved bye. OK, here goes.

I started to walk in. I looked down at my feet. I looked around for my Mom. I took my slippers off and stuffed them in my bag.

And it looked ... beautiful!!!!!

It was even better than I imagined it! I walked into a big room ...

The sign said:

Welcome to the Ball!
WELCOME PRINCESSES!

And this is what I saw. Everything was silver and pink! Like streamers and balloons everywhere! And a big poster of a castle. And a sparkly disco ball! There was a big pink and silver throne up on a stage.

Wow, wow, and wow!

"Maddy!" It was Kacey! And Isabel! And Claire! They came running over!

"Where are your shoes?" Claire asked.

"OK, there was this little accident," I said. "No biggie. I don't need shoes."

"Doesn't this place look so pretty? Isn't it like a real ball? Don't you feel like a real princess?" Kacey said. She was bouncing all over.

Yes, yes, and yes!

"Lauren said to put your stuff over by that door," Isabel pointed. And then we can go meet her. And find out what we're going to be doing."

I walked back over to the front door. I put my bag down. And then I saw her.

MOM! Looking at my bare feet!

Uh.

Oh.

chapter 8

"Maddy!" she said. "Your overnight supplies bag fell out in the car. You forgot it." She looked down.

"Looks like you also forgot your slippers."

"Uh ..." I said. "But they don't match!" Plus they look way stupid!

But Mom was looking at me like NOW.

OK, OK. Whatever. I put on my slippers. She gave me a kiss goodbye. I went back over to the TOO Crew.

"OK, I know. I'm wearing dumb slippers," I said. "I can't help it."

"I think they're fun!" Kacey said.

"I think they're cute!" Claire said.

"I think they're YOU!" Isabel said.

"If you feel uncomfortable, you want to borrow my slippers?" Claire offered. That girl is way generous!

But my feet are way bigger than all of theirs.

Anyway, Lauren came over to us.

"Girls!" Lauren said. "Welcome to the Royal Sleepover! Your job? First, check in the girls. After that? Try out everything and have fun. And we'll meet tomorrow to share the results "

Music started cranking! ♪ ♪ ♪

And the girls started coming in!

"Welcome to the Royal Sleepover!" we said. "Hi! Welcome! Come in!"

The girls were excited! They were like, "Hi! Hi! Thanks! Yay!"

I was checking names off a list like crazy!

✓Caitie   ✓Savannah   ✓Lisa   ✓Kara

"Hi, welcome to the Royal Sleepover!" I said.

✓Kristin   ✓Sydney   ✓Naya   ✓Chloe

"Hello? I mean, are we going to get in this place or what?" a girl said. "I'm Piper. But don't even bother to check. I'm on every list."

Piper? I looked up.

"Oh, it's YOU."

PIPER! With her friend. Sierra. And two other girls.

"We get tickets to everything," Sierra said. "Because Piper's father? Major connections."

Blugh.

"Check out those slippers," Piper said, looking at my feet. "Are you the frog that the princess kisses? And then you become a prince?"

My face? Totally bright red.

"NEXT," Isabel said loudly. "Please do not hold up the line."

√Piper   √Sierra   √Traci   √Brandi

They moved on.

Whew.

Some more girls came through. They seemed way excited!!! Not like Piper and her friends who were like, blah blah we're too kewl.

√ Allison   √ Amber   √ Ami   √ Andi

Wait a minute. That sounded familiar.

I looked up. The girls from the car wash! Who were in town for ... an event!

"Oh hi!" I said. "You're the four A's! I met you at the car wash!"

"Oh hiiiiii!" they said.

"You're Maddy, right?" one of the girls said.

"Yeah! You remembered!"

"You were so nice to us!"

"I hope you guys have fun tonight," I told them.

"We always have fun together!" one of them said.

Those girls were so smiley. They reminded me of Kacey! Four Kaceys!

We got all the girls checked in.

Lauren was up on stage. We heard her over a microphone.

"Welcome, girls," she said. "Thank you for coming to the Princess Pajama Party! Please feel free to visit the royal testing area. Have fun!"

Majestic Makeovers

"Welcome, girls," another woman said. "We'd like to ask your opinion here. Our company is planning to make some new kinds of lip glosses. So if you would try these on and rate them for us! 1-10 and 10 is the highest!"

Sure! Just like my diary!

I tried on these lip glosses:

- ☆ Root beer fizzy - 7 (Yum! Like root beer, but too sticky.)
- ☆ Raz Berrylicious - 3 (Eh. Sparkles are too crazy.)
- ☆ Smores - 10 (Super Yum! I liked the shiny part.)
- ☆ Cinnamon red-hot - 1 (Too strong! Made my lips too dark.)
- ☆ Vanilla ice cream - 9 (Yum! And I like the sparkles in this.)

Then the woman let me pick one to keep (Smores).

"Would you like a princess makeover?" the woman asked.

"Yes!"

"We have a selection of princessy colors," the woman said. "Would you like me to choose?"

"Sure!"

She dusted sparkle powder on my nose.

Some light purply eye shadow on my eyes.

A little pale pink blush on my cheeks.

And some stuff to cover up a zit.

And tada!

I looked in the mirror. I looked pretty good! For me, anyway!

I went to see the rest of the TOO Crew. They all got their makeovers, too! Way pretty!

"Which color did you guys pick?" I asked them.

"Root beer fizzy!" Kacey said. "I like it all sticky!"

"I'm wearing the raspberry," Isabel said. "I thought the glitter looked cool."

"And I liked the vanilla," Claire said. "It's so sweet."

"That's so funny," I said. "We are totally picking different things!!! I hated that cinnamon one, though."

"Ooo ya!" Kacey said. "Me, too!"

"Yeah, yuk!" Isabel said.

"Way too spicy," Claire agreed.

"Nobody likes the cinnamon?"

Oh! The woman from the lip gloss company.

"Oh, sorry," I said. "I didn't mean to talk bad about your stuff."

"Honey, that's why we're here. To hear what you have to say," the woman said. "It looks like we will be needing to tweak our cinnamon. Good thing we have these focus groups!"

Enchanted Hairdos

"Welcome," a woman told us. "No opinions needed, just fun hairstyles!"

We got to pick a fancy style for our hair!

- ★ Fairy Tale Princess! Up in a fancy knot!
- ★ Glam Princess! Wavy and decorated with glitter sparkles!
- ★ Mermaid Princess! Braids and flowers stuck in it!
- ★ Pop Star Princess! Your hair like a rocker princess with color streaks!

I had to make a choice!

I picked the Mermaid Princess!

The woman put little braids in my hair. Then she looped them up. And stuck little flowers in them. She held up a mirror.

CUTE!!!!

"Maddy! That looks sooo cool!" Kacey came running over. She had picked the Pop Star Princess. Her hair had little twists all over it. With a bright pink streak!

"You look awesome!" I told her.

Claire came over! Looking way pretty as a Fairy Tale Princess! She had her hair twisted up in a ballerina bun. With pink sparkly bow barrettes!

Isabel came over. She chose the Glam Princess. She had her hair all wavy and piled up on her head. And there were silver glitter sparkles on it!

We are sooo princesses!

"Hi Maddy!" It was the 4 A's! They all had their hair done in matching Fairy Tale Princess style.

"Hi guys!" I said. I introduced them to the TOO Crew.

"Love the hair," Isabel said. "It looks like Claire's."

"Allison picked it," Amber said. "We're letting her pick everything tonight. She's the contest winner!"

"You guys DON'T have to do that," laughed Allison.

"Well, you made a good choice with the hair," Isabel said.

"I picked Fairy Tale Princess because this night is like a fairy tale!" Allison said. "I never won anything before!"

"See you guys later!" Amber said. We all waved bye.

Princess Pampering

We get to have our nails done!!!!

"I love manicures," Claire said. "My father's girlfriend has been taking me with her to the salon."

"I never get real ones like that," I said.

"Me either!" said Kacey.

"That's no problem," the woman said. "But while you're waiting, we could use your help. Would you like to make up some names for nail polishes?"

Oooh! Fun!

The woman gave us each a few colors.Here's what I thought:

⭐ Princess Power Pink
⭐ Lady of the Castle Lavender
⭐ Glass Slipper Silver
⭐ Queen Bluish-Green

"I usually wear pink so I'm going to do something different,"
I said. I chose the Queen Bluish-green!

"Turquoise is pretty. So are you having fun?" the manicurist
asked.

"Yeah!" I said. "This is so cool!"

The TOO Crew ran over. We all held up our fingers.

Claire's were pink!

Isabel's were lavender!

Kacey's were silver!

And mine were turquoise!

FANCY!!!!!!

chapter 9

Charmed Candy

"Welcome, girls!" a woman said. "Our company is testing different kinds of candy. Feel free to take a piece of each kind. And rate them for us!"

I tried a dark red gummy thing.

AHHHHHHHH! My mouth is on fire!!!!!!!

"OK!" I said. "I'm so NOT into the hot spicy thing here!"

I wrote down: 1

"Really?" Kacey asked, chewing. "I kinda like it." She popped another one in her mouth. And wrote something down.

I tested some different candies. Here's my list:

★ Sour apple crunchy - 7
★ Cotton candy flavored fluffy - 9
★ Banana swirly lollipop - 5
★ Chewy green and red wormy - 10
★ Black licorice hard candy - 2

Then they asked me to rank different kinds of candy. Worst to best! Here's my list:

- ☆ Black licorice
- ☆ Lollipops
- ☆ Candy corn
- ☆ Jelly beans
- ☆ Chocolate

And my fave candy is ...

Gummy anything!!!

"So gummy candy is your favorite?" the woman asked. And handed me a big bag of gummy spiders. Mmm! Yummy!

I saw the rest of the TOO Crew still trying candy.

I started to walk over to them. But then the 4 A girls came over to me!

"Hi Maddy!" they said.

"Are you guys having fun?" I asked them. Amber and Ami were eating chocolate bars. Andi and Allison were eating gummy candy like me!

They were all like, "YEAH!"

"So have you been friends with those guys for a long time?" Amber asked me. She pointed to the TOO Crew.

"Not that long," I said. "Just before school started."

I told them how I met the TOO Crew in the girl's bathroom at the mall! And how we became the TOO Crew!

They were like, "No way!"

"I'm thirsty," Allison said. "I'll bring back some bottles of water!"

"So you guys been friends a long time?" I asked.

"Since we were born!" Ami said. "Isn't that crazy? Our moms became friends at this 'Getting ready for baby' class!"

"And they named us all A names!" Amber said.

"And we've been best friends always," Andi said.

"That is really wild," I said. "That is so cool you all got to come tonight."

"Yeah, we were so excited for Allison when we found out she won," Ami said. "And then we found out she could take us. We were like eeeeee!"

They gave each other a high-five.

"Allison really needed this right now," Amber said.

Then they all of a sudden looked serious. Seriously serious.

"Her parents are getting a divorce," Ami said. "And it's been really bad."

Wow. That's really sad

"She's been so bummed!" Amber said. "We were hoping tonight would cheer her up!"

"And it is!" Andi said. "She's like the old smiley Allison tonight!"

Allison came back over with bottles of water.

"We were just telling Maddy about your parents," Amber said. "Hope that's OK."

"Yeah," she sighed. "It's really sad."

"Well, if you need someone good to talk to," I told her. "I bet Isabel would help. She's good at stuff like that. And her parents got divorced, too."

"Thanks," Allison said.

The 3 A's hugged her.

"Have some of my chocolate!" Andi said.

Those girls were way nice friends!!!

And then my friends came over. Kacey was eating jelly beans, Claire was eating candy corn, and Isabel was eating a ring lollipop.

"Do we like ANYTHING the same?" I said. We were cracking up!!!

Royal T-Shirts

"Hi, I'm representing a t-shirt design company. This area has two parts," the woman explained. "First, make your own t-shirt design! Second, vote for your favorite t-shirt design from all of these pictures."

She gave us these special markers. We could draw anything we wanted on the white t-shirt.

"I bet I know what Maddy is drawing," Isabel said. "Something with a dog on it!"

"Yup!" I said. I drew a cute little foofy dog. Who looked like Buggie! Then I put a princess crown on her head. Tada! Princess Lovebug. OK, the dog looked a little goofy. I am so not a great artist.

Kacey drew a ... uh ... uh ...

"Can you tell what this is supposed to be?" she asked.

"Um," I said. I didn't want to hurt her feelings. "A banana?"

"Oops!" Kacey laughed. "I tried. A magic wand!"

"Sorry," I said. "I mean, I didn't mean to hurt your feelings!"

"Ohmigosh," she said, all smiley. "About a picture? No way! I am so not the best artist!"

Claire drew a castle with a rainbow over it. It was pretty.

"Wow, check out Isabel's," I said. Hers was ... GORGEOUS! She drew this unicorn that looked real!

"That is so amazing!" Kacey said.

"You are seriously talented," Claire said.

"Thanks, you guys," Isabel said.

Isabel wants to be a fashion designer someday! I think she could practically be one now!

Then we got to pick our fave designs from some samples hanging up. There were all kinds of designs!

I picked one with two puppies on it!

Kacey picked one with a smiley face!

Claire picked one with butterflies!

Isabel picked one with a Hawaii-style print!

"They're cool! And Isabel! I think yours is as good as any of those!" I said.

"Thanks, Maddy!" she said.

Music for the Ball

OK! We had our next area to go to. The music area.

"Hello, girls," a woman said. "You may have heard about a new movie coming out ..."

"YES!" squealed Kacey. "With Carter McLain!"

"We totally can't wait for this movie," I told her.

"Well, we'd love to hear what you think of some songs," she said. "We're considering them for the movie soundtrack."

She gave us each a pair of headphones. I plugged mine in and listened.

I was listening to the first song when I looked up. It was good!
I was dancing a little bit.

And saw Piper and Sierra. With their two friends.

They were pointing at my feet again. At my frog slippers.

OK. So they were in little kitten heels. I was in frog slippers.
Get over it!!!!

That's what I felt like saying.

Instead I hid my feet. 'Cuz I felt STUPID!!!

chapter 10

I turned around and listened to the songs. And then I felt way better. Because one of the songs was by Carter McLain!

"OK, is that Carter McLain?" I asked. "I didn't know he could sing!"

"Yes," said the woman. "He actually came out to Hollywood to pursue a singing career. And got into acting first."

Hm! He was a good singer! His song was about finding the right person!

Way romantic. Sigh.

So anyway.

I told the woman I liked it. Then she put another song on for me.

I recognized these singers, too!

"Hey! That's INSPIRE!" I said. "My fave group! Are they going to be on the movie CD? That would be awesome!"

I didn't know that! It didn't say so on their fan site! I check it all the time!

"It might be!" the woman said. "I'll add your vote!"

Claire came over.

"Did you hear INSPIRE's new song?" I asked. "That sounded so great."

"Yes!" she said. "And Carter McLain's song was really good, too."

"Hey!" Kacey came over. "Did you guys know INSPIRE had a song in this movie?"

Before we could answer, we heard someone say,

"You guys didn't know that?"

Piper.

"I thought you guys knew everything about INSPIRE. I thought you were like, close personal friends with them. Even I knew that."

"Piper's father is in the music business," said Sierra. "So she knows EVERYTHING."

"Whatever," Kacey said. "Let's go somewhere else."

We walked away.

"Ribbit," I heard.

I know that was about my slippers.

I looked at Kacey and Claire. They didn't hear it. I would pretend I didn't, too! Isabel came over with us.

"OK," she said. "We have one area left. It's the ..."

Gowns for the Ball

"Welcome," a woman said. "Please choose a gown of your liking."

And this is what I saw:

- ★ Bunches of ball gowns!
- ★ All different colors and styles!!!
- ★ Not like little kid dress up stuff!!
- ★ Like go to the ball drop dead GORGEOUS dresses!

WOW!

"Check these out!" Kacey said dancing around the racks. "These are incredible!"

It was so hard to choose! I saw Kacey, Isabel and Claire pick out their dresses. I couldn't choose!

Then Lauren came over.

"Girls," Lauren was talking to Isabel. She waved us over. "How's it going?"

We looked around. Everyone was totally having fun! Looking way glam! They were smiling!

"Great!" Kacey said. "Way fun!"

"I think we're going to be wrapping this part up soon," Lauren said. "So I could use your help in just a few minutes."

Ack! I need to pick!

"Help!" I told Isabel. Isabel is really good at knowing what looks good.

"Hm, with your hairstyle, I'd go with that one," Isabel said.

She pointed to a turquoise blue long dress. It was all shimmery and poufed out at the bottom. Like a Mermaid Princess!

I went into a dressing room. I tried it on. Sooooo pretty!

Only one problem. It wasn't long enough to cover my slippers. Did I have time to change?

"Maddy," Isabel said. "Lauren needs us."

Nope.

I came out. Everyone was all dressed up wayyyy pretty.

Kacey was wearing a hot pink dress with sequin sparkles. It was shorter and went Pouf! Around her knees. It matched her Pop Star Princess hair!

Isabel was wearing a long white gown that was kinda straight up and down. It had diamonds on the edges. And she had a white feather boa! Way Glam Princess!

Claire was wearing a light pink dress that poufed out. She had on long white gloves. She looked sooo Fairy Tale Princess!

"Maddy, you look so beautiful," Claire said.

I looked in the mirror. I looked like a real princess! I looked around. All these girls were all in their pink and yellow and blue and white dresses.

I saw Andi, Allison and Ami from the 4 A's.

"You guys look so nice!" I said. They were in matching style dresses.

"You picked everything the same again!" I blurted out. "Do

you guys always like the same things?"

I mean, me and the TOO Crew picked everything different practically! We were soooo different.

"Nope," Ami said. "Just tonight."

"We let Allison pick everything tonight," Andi said. "She's like our Queen tonight!"

Then Amber came over. She was still wearing her shirt and pants from before?

"See?" Ami said. "We don't always do everything the same!"

"Yah, I hate wearing dresses!" Amber said. "I didn't really want to dress up. I mean, it's just not me."

"So I told her I don't care! She can do whatever she wants," Allison said. "Amber looks great in anything!"

"Isn't Allison soooo sweet?" Ami said.

"Yay Allison for bringing us tonight!" Andi cheered.

Allison got pretty blushy.

"Cut it out, you guys," she said. "Of COURSE I would bring you. I'm getting a drink."

She walked away.

"Did we embarrass her?" I asked.

"Just in a good way!" Amber said, all cheerful.

"We're just sooo happy to see Allison happy tonight," Ami said. "She's been so sad. We tried everything to cheer her up! But it's working tonight!"

"You guys are seriously together-friends," I said.

"We're really lucky," Ami agreed.

Lauren was announcing something. It was time for the ...

chapter 11

Rags to Riches Scavenger Hunt

"Attention, girls," Lauren announced. "You all look fabulous. Let's get started on the Rags to Riches Scavenger Hunt!"

This is what we had to do!

- ☆ We would be given a list and a sticker camera.
- ☆ We would have to do the stuff on the list. The people in the mall would be there to help.
- ☆ We would take sticker photos of our team completing the list.
- ☆ Whichever team brings the finished list back first ... wins!

"Oh, we will so ROCK this!" I heard Piper say. She high-fived her friends.

Anyway. How fun is this?! We all got our lists. Ready, Go?

I wrote our team name on the top of our list.

TEAM TOO CREW!

"What's on the list!?" Kacey shrieked. I read it out loud.

#1. RAGS: Find four things that Cinderella would use to clean her stepmother's home. And pretend to be Cinderella in rags.

"Let's go to the store with all the kitchen thingies in it!" Kacey said, all bouncing all over the place.

"Let's gooooo!" We screamed. We ran out and into the mall. There were Princess girls running everywhere to all kinds of stores. (And then we were told to walk.)

We walked super fast! And made it to a housewares store! There was a woman there. To make sure we didn't abuse the merchandise, I guess.

"OK, we need four things Cinderella would use!" Isabel said.

"A mop!" Kacey grabbed a mop.

"A sponge!" Isabel said, taking one.

"An apron!" Claire said, running to the aprons.

"How about a broom?" I said.

"Get a picture!!!" Kacey shrieked.

We stood together. Kacey mopped the floor! Isabel sponged my head. Claire put on the apron. I mopped. We all made really,

really sad faces. Like a sad Cinderella in rags.

The mall lady took our picture with a sticker camera.

"Thank you!" we screamed. I stuck the photo on the card. Hey, it was kinda cute. We all looked very sad and cleaning-ish. Hee.

"Hurry, what's next on the list, Maddy!?" Claire asked. Oh!

#2. MICE: Cinderella was friends with the mice. Go make friends with some mice.

"Mice?" Kacey shrieked. "Eeek!"

"Oh, you're scared of mice?" Claire asked. "They run around my horse's stall all the time. Don't worry."

We looked at her like really? Because Claire seems so princessy and girly! But she's not scared of things!

"Let's go to the pet store!" Isabel said. "Come on!"

We all ran to the pet store! The woman there said we just had to take a picture next to the cage.

"Whew! That's friendly enough for me," Kacey said.

We all ran up to the cage of mice.

"OK, they're kinda cute!" I said. We stuck our faces next to the cage.

\- CLICK! \-

The woman took a picture. I stuck it to the card next to #2. We were ready for ...

#3. Your fairy godmother can help you get to the ball. Go find your own fairy godmother.

"What's that supposed to mean?" Kacey asked.

We looked around. All these Princess girls were zooming all over like crazy! We had to hurry!!!!

"Lauren's kind of like our fairy godmother," Claire said. But we didn't think that was it.

We were stumped.

"OK, let's think out of the box," Isabel said.

"Um, huh?" I said.

"Think creatively. We are supposed to find our own fairy godmother," Isabel said.

"I have an idea!" Claire said. She waved us to come on! We all took off after her. She ran over to Build-A-Bear Workshop. We ran inside.

Claire pointed to the wall. To a costume of a fairy!

"I get it!" I said. "We dress up a bear like a fairy!"

We asked the woman working there. She said, "Go for it!"

"Or a bunny," Kacey said, picking up a stuffed rabbit.

"Or a unicorn," I said, holding up a white unicorn.

"Ooooh, that's cute," Kacey said.

"OK guys! Hellooo? We're trying to hurry!" Isabel reminded us.

Whoops! Scavenger hunt!

We all ran and got fairy stuff. Wings, a wand, platform sandals ....

"Platform sandals?" I said.

"OK, I got carried away," Isabel said. "I think a fairy godmother would be hip in platform sandals."

Isabel is so a fashion designer! She dressed the unicorn.

"Here she is, our fairy godmother," Claire held the unicorn up.

We all scrunched together.

"Here, we should look like we're asking her something," I said. I clasped my hands together like I was begging. Everyone clasped their hands together, too.

CLICK!

The woman took our picture.

chapter 12

I stuck the sticker photo on our card!

"Bye, fairy godmother Unicorn," Kacey waved. Because we had to check out our next clue!

#4. Your fairy godmother is ready to prepare you for the ball. Go find your perfect princess accessories at Limited TOO.

"Let's go!" Isabel said. We raced down the hall! Around the corner! To Limited TOO.

"Hi girls," the woman said when we ran in.

"We're here to find our Princess accessories!" I told her.

"Hi TOO Crew!!"

The 4 A's were in there, too!

"We found our princess accessories!" Ami said.

"Now we're stumped," Allison said. "Our next clue is something about a fairy godmother."

"Think creatively," advised Isabel.

"Good luck!" we all yelled. We looked all over the store and found our princess accessories.

Kacey found a necklace with a princess charm.

Claire found a little purse with a princess crown on it!

Isabel found a bracelet that said Princess!

And I found a shirt with a dog wearing a princess crown!

We all pretended to be wearing our accessories. The woman took our picture.

CLICK!

I stuck the sticker photo on the paper.

"This is really cute," Claire said, looking inside the purse. "I wonder if I can buy it, now."

"Claire!" we all said. "Later! We have to hurry!!!"

OK! Our next clue was:

#5. Find your perfect princess glass slipper.

"Oh great, grab a shoe!" I said, pointing to a shoe stand.

"Actually, I think the rule is you have to go to a different store for everything," the woman said.

OK! We yelled thanks to the woman. And took off! We knew where to go! The shoe store!

Shoes!

We all grabbed a shoe we liked.

Kacey grabbed a white sneaker with sparkles.

Claire grabbed a little pink shoe with heels

Isabel grabbed a funky chunky platform sandal.

"Uh ..." I didn't know what to grab.

"Pick something, Maddy!" everyone yelled. I looked around. Ummmmm ... Oh! Perfect! A little white ballerina slipper.

We all pretended to try on our shoe. We posed and ...

CLICK! The woman took our picture.

"Too bad the store is closed," I said. "I could buy some shoes. So I don't have to wear these dumb slippers."

"Maddy, they're cute," Isabel said. "Move on."

"OK, OK, what's next?" Kacey said.

#6. Cinderella's pumpkin turned into a coach. First, find your pumpkin.

Hm. Tough one.

"A Halloween store?" I suggested.

"Wrong season," Isabel said. "Hm ... Something pumpkin-y."

"How about a candle store? My father's girlfriend loves pumpkin spice candles when she relaxes in her hot tub," Claire said.

"Great idea!" Isabel said. "Let's go!"

We ran to the candle store.

Cinnamon, rainy day, mango ... aha! Pumpkin!

We grabbed the pumpkin candle and held it up. The woman in the store took our picture.

 CLICK!

"Almost done" I said. "Just two more! The next clue is ...

#7. You found your pumpkin. It now turns into a coach. Find your fanciest ride to the ball.

"The car store!" Kacey squealed.

"Um, I don't think there's a car store in the mall," I pointed out.

"Oh yeah!" Kacey said. "OK! How about the toy store! With all the little cars!"

"Great idea!" Isabel said. We took off for the toy store!

We passed all these Princess girls racing all over! We ran into the toy store!

"OK, a fancy coach," I said. I ran past the bikes and ... Hee. I grabbed a tricycle. And started riding around the store.

It was so little! My knees were bumping into my chin!

"Maddy, that's too funny," Claire said.

"Please don't insult my magic coach," I told her. "Only the classiest of princesses take the ..." I checked the name on the bike. "... Kutesy Kiddy Trike to the ball."

"Oh, that's too funny," Claire said. "I want a ride like Maddy's." She got on a trike, too!

And then Kacey grabbed one of those giant balls you sit on and hold the handle. Bounce! Bounce!

"Look at meee!" Kacey said. "I'm going to the ball on my hopping ball!"

"AHEM!" the woman at the store spoke. "Girls! I am afraid this is a violation of store policy."

Oopsie. BUSTED.

"I'm afraid I will have to ask you two to remove yourselves from the tricycles. There is a size limit. You will need to all bounce like crazy on hoppy balls like that girl."

Hee! OK! I grabbed a blue one! Kacey was on a red! Isabel was on an orange! And Claire was on a yellow. Boing! Bounce!

We were bouncing like crazy all over the store! HEE!

"Sooo immature," I heard someone walk in and say.

Piper! Piper and her team were looking at us.

I stopped bouncing. I felt kinda stupid.

"I knew that girl was babyish," Piper's friend named Brandi whispered to Sierra. "I mean, look at her slippers."

My face started turning red. But Isabel was totally like ... Oh puh-lease. I'm not going to let you guys ruin our fun!

"Lighten up, Piper," Isabel said. "Have a little fun in your life."

And Isabel bounced away. And kept bouncing! I started bouncing again! Higher! Boing! Bounce!

Piper was all rolling her eyes. But Sierra goes, "Oh, cool!" She grabbed a hoppy ball like Kacey's. But she only got to hop once!

"Sierra!" Piper said. "Come ON!"

"But that looks fun," Sierra was whining. Piper and Brandi and the other girl, I forget her name, dragged her away.

Poor Sierra. Look what she has to deal with!

"Our photo!" Kacey said. We all smushed together on our "coaches." The woman at the front took our picture.

CLICK!

We ran and put our stuff back.

"OK you guys!" I said. "This is our very last clue!"

#8. Go find your favorite princess story. And then we've "booked" you for reservations to the ball.

"Booked us?" Kacey said.

"The bookstore!" We hit the mall! We waved HI! to other Princess teams! We waved hi! to the 4 A's!

"We're on our last clue!" Ami called out.

"Us, too!" I yelled!

We found it! The bookstore!

We all went in. "Find your fave princess story!" I called out.

"Got it!" Kacey yelled. She held up a beauty and the beast one. Isabel held a classic one about a little princess. Claire found a newish book about an enchanted Cinderella. And I grabbed the one where a girl found out she's a princess.

"Picture time!" Claire said. We all opened our books. We pretended to read them. And the woman took our picture.

CLICK!

I stuck the sticker on the page.

"Are we done?" Isabel asked me.

I looked at the directions. We were supposed to go back to the sleepover room.

"GO!" I screamed. We took off! We walked past the stationery store! The food court! The computer store.

"Out of our way!" PIPER! And her team.

"We're finished," Sierra said.

"So are we!" Kacey said.

"We're finished first," Piper and her friends pushed right past us.

"We're gonna win." Piper said. We were all like, hurry, hurry. And then ...

Piper walked behind me. And she stepped on the back of my slipper.

WHOA!!!!!

I lost my balance! And I flopped forward! I fell on the ground! OOF!!!

"Maddy!" Everyone was all, "Are you OK?"

Piper and her team walked really fast ahead of us.

"I'm OK," I told them. "She stepped on my slipper."

"That girl is so rude," Claire said.

"I'm OK, let's keep going." I got up. I felt all stupid, though.

"If she does anything else to you, we're telling Lauren," Isabel said.

We got to the door. Lauren was standing there. Piper and her team were handing her their card.

"Done!" Piper said, smiling all sweet.

"Congratulations," Lauren said. "Head on inside to collect your riches."

Did Piper and her team WIN?!!!

chapter 13

"Hi TOO Crew!" Lauren said. "Let's see your card."

She looked at the sticker photos.

"Oh, look at you on the hoppy balls and things," she smiled. "Oh, your fairy godmother is very clever. And cute!"

We all smiled.

"Congratulations," she said. She gave me back the card. "Head on inside for the festivities."

"Here are your riches," a woman said. She handed us each a colorful bag.

"Goodie bags!" Kacey squealed.

With lip gloss! Candy! Body glitter! A hair thingy! A purple book! A CD!

COOL!!!

We went in. And we saw ... the 4 A's! And like 5 other teams of girls! We didn't win! (But neither did Piper, heh!)

And we also saw ...

A DJ at a table! And a dance floor! It was time for ...

THE BALL!!!

All the Princess girls came inside! Lauren went up on a stage and talked over a microphone.

"Thank you girls for helping give your opinions tonight," Lauren said. "We've still got a lot of fun. And now, welcome to the Royal Ball!"

Then all of a sudden, the lights dimmed. And then colored lights started flashing. We looked up. A huge disco ball was sparkling!

DANCE PARTY!!! ♩ ♪ ♩ ♩ ♩ ♩

Dance music cranked from speakers all over the room. Everyone was like YEAH!!! Everyone was dancing!

"I love this song!" Isabel said.

"How cool is this!" Kacey squealed. A gajillion girls looking like princesses! Dancing all around.

OK, I'm kinda not the greatest dancer, right? Especially in big fluffy slippers? But this was perfect! It was kinda dark! So nobody could really see me! So I was dancing like crazy!!!

"Oops!" I bumped into someone. "Sorry!"

"That's OK, Maddy!" It was one of the 4 A's! I started dancing with them in a circle.

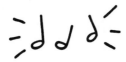

Kacey and Isabel and Claire started dancing with us!

"Ready for a line dance?" the DJ announced.

Some people were like YEAH!

I was like ... maybe! OK! Because sometimes it's like everyone else knows the dance! And I don't! So I have to stand and watch. And my friends are always, come on, Maddy! Just come on and try it! But I always feel dumb! And left out!

"The Slide!" the DJ announced.

Yay! I know this one! The music started!

We all went out and were like ... Left foot, right foot, bend, twist, clap!

I looked around. Tons of Princess girls! Hopping and clapping and twisting and bending!

SOOOOOO COOL!!!

"I need to get some water!" Allison said next to me. "Be right back."

Dancin!

Dance party!

We finished up the Slide. Everyone was like YEAH!

And then ...

I saw Allison.

And she was crying!

"Allison!" Amber said to the other A's. They all ran over to her.

"I hope she's OK," I said. I was worried. Allison was so happy before!

She looked like she was crying.

"I'm going to quick ask if we can help," Isabel said. She went over. And then she came back mad.

"Allison said she was waiting in line," Isabel told us. "And some girl said some really mean stuff to her. Making fun of her."

"That's so wrong!" Kacey said.

"I feel bad for her," Claire said.

"I wish she didn't let that girl bother her," said Isabel.

Isabel was soo cool! If someone was rude to her she was like huh! Well, that's their problem. She ignored it. I was trying to be like that! But ..not always working.

I saw the 4 A's head to the bathroom. Amber turned around and waved at us. Like, she'll be OK.

I looked around. Everyone else was having sooooo much fun!

Then I saw the 4 A's come back out on the dance floor. Allison was smiling. They started dancing. Phew.

Then the music stopped.

"We're going to take a little break," Lauren announced. "Please help yourself to snacks. And in a few minutes, we will announce this evening's winner of the PRINCESS PRIZE!"

Lauren came over.

"Hi girls, I thought you could help out," she said. "I need to take care of something. If one of you could announce the winning team for the scavenger hunt I would appreciate it."

"Sure!" We all said.

But. Pick someone besides me! I thought. 'Cuz talking onstage? Made me way nervous!!!

Isabel should do it. She's always way confident. Talking on stage? No big deal for her!

Or maybe Kacey. She'd get so excited. She'd get everyone psyched up!!!

Or Claire! She's so princess-y! She'd be perfect.

"I drew an X on one of these pieces of paper," Lauren said. "Whoever picks the X will announce." She held out her hands.

We all picked! Uncrumpled our paper.

Mine had the X. I won. Or, in my case ... lost! Because ...

I looked around. There were like a bajillion girls here! And there would be two bajillion eyes staring at me onstage!

Yup. Definitely nervousing.

"Um," I said. "I don't mind if someone else wants to do this."

"Maddy you won fair and square," Kacey said. "We couldn't take it away from you."

"It's going to be so exciting!" Claire said. "You'll actually get to make some girls tonight's Prize Princesses!"

Um ... but ...

 "I know you're nervous, Maddy," Isabel said. "But it's good for you. The more you talk onstage the better you get at it!"

Rats.

Oooo-K! Lauren told me what I was supposed to say. And then ... pull yourself together Maddy. It's time. I went up onstage.

chapter 14

"OK, can you hear me?" I said into the microphone. "Um, hi. I'm Maddy and ..."

SCREEEEEEEEEEE!!!!!!!!

The microphone made this noise like ...

SCREEEEEEEEEEEEEEEEEEEEEEEEEEEEEEEEEEEEEEEE!

OK like the worst noise ever! Everyone in the audience was like Ack! Cover your ears!

SCREEEEEEEEEEEEEEEEEEEEEEEEEEEEEEEEEEEEEEEEEEE
EEEEEEEEEEEEEEEEEEEEEEEEEEEEEEEEEEEEEEEEEEEE!

OK, OK, OK how do I turn this thing off!!!

"That noise is giving me a headache!" I heard Sierra whine.

Isabel came running over. She did something to the microphone and ...

Whew!

The screeching stopped! Everyone stopped plugging their

ears so they could listen.

But I couldn't say anything.

Red-face Rating: ☆★☆★☆ out of ☆★☆★☆ stars.
I was supposed to talk! Not the microphone!

Then I saw Piper whispering to Sierra. They were pointing at me. And giggling. Then their friends started giggling.

OK, the microphone thing? So over!

Why are they cracking up?

Then I looked down.

Oh.

I was wearing my beautiful gown! My fancy hair! My sparkly makeup!

And my huge bright green fluffy frog slippers.

The ones Brittany was laughing at! The ones Piper and her friends were laughing at. The ones probably every single girl in the audience was laughing at, too.

AUGH!!!!

But OK. I look like a Major Dork. Get me OFF THIS STAGE!

But the TOO Crew was like, Go Maddy Go!

Recover, Maddy, recover.

I started talking.

"The winning team will get to go on the Perfect Princess Limo ride tonight. There will be a prize basket full of goodies in it!"

Everyone was like OOOOOOhhhh!

Because riding in a limo? SWEET!

And the winning team is ... I opened the envelope.

"The 4 A's! Allison, Amber, Ami and Andi!"

They were like EEEEEEEEEEEEEEEEEEE!!!! Yay! The 4 A's won! They ran up onstage.

"Ohmigosh!" they were all jumping around. "We're soooo excited!"

"Can I say something into the microphone?" Ami asked.

"Sure," I said. "I think so." I handed it to her.

"Hi everybody," Ami said. "We're so psyched to win this. And I also wanted to say something. I'm especially psyched for our friend Allison."

Allison was like HUH?

"She brought us tonight and I just wanted to thank her. And let everyone know she is the greatest person and she is like a true princess. Thank you."

Everyone was like aaaaww. That was soo nice! The 4 A's were all hugging!

Oh! Allison started crying!

"Are you OK?" I asked her.

"I'm just soo ... soo ... happy!!!!!" she said.

YAY! HAPPY CRYING!!!

Everybody was clapping!

Those girls are so nice. I'm glad they won.

 I went down the steps. The 4 A's started to follow me. And then we heard this ...

"Excuse me, I need the winning team to come on back onstage."

It was Lauren.

"We have one more surprise for you. We're hoping you wouldn't mind an extra guest in the limo. Me, as your chaperone. And ...

"Our surprise guest ... movie star and singer, Carter McLain!"

And out walked ...

CARTER MCLAIN!!!!

AHHHHHHHHHHHHHHHHHHHHHHHHH!!!!!!!

Everyone was like ... AHHHHHHHH! Screaming and all crazy!

Because I mean, Carter McLain! A real live celebrity! In true and real life!!!

That WAS him Brittany saw in that limo! And now the 4 A's are going to drive around in that limo with Carter McLain!

OK! How lucky are those girls tonight!!!!!!

Carter McLain walked over to the 4 A's and said hi. And they were like ...

Oh. My. GOSH!!!!!!!!!! AHHHHH!! The real person of Carter McLain!

Allison was smiling the biggest smile ever when she walked offstage!

"And we have another surprise," Lauren said. "Carter McLain will perform two of the songs from his movie that's coming out ..."

And everyone went ...

AHHHHHHHHHHHHHHHHHHHHHHHHHHHHHHHHHHHHHH!!!!!!!

The lights got low. The music came on.

Carter McLain took the microphone.

"Hello, Princesses," he said. "I'd like to sing a song in honor of tonight's Princess Party. It's called *'Tonight You are My Princess.'*"

We were all like ... Ahhhhhhhhhhh. He's sooo cute!

And then Carter goes ...

"This is a song about a prince who has found his perfect princess. So I'd like to pick one special princess to come up here and join me."

This spotlight came on. And went all around the audience.

"Check out, Piper," Kacey whispered.

Piper was all quick putting on lipstick. And posing. And looking like, me, pick me, pick me.

And then Carter McLain goes, "Reporters always ask me what my perfect girl would be like. I tell them my perfect girl has a good sense of humor. She is unique and stands out from the crowd ..."

Everyone was like ... WHO IS IT? PICK ME! PICK ME!!

Then Carter goes, "Some princesses wear glass slippers. But I like my princess to wear FROG slippers."

The spotlight stopped on ... ME.

Uh. Huh?

Wait. OK what is going on?!! Is Carter McLain making fun of my slippers?

"I grew up on a farm," Carter was saying. "And I always had a pet frog ..."

"Maddy! It's you! He picked you!" Kacey was all jumpy all over the place!

"How exciting!" Claire said.

"Go on, Maddy!" Isabel said. She gave me a little push.

But I stood there.

"Maddy, he LIKES your frog slippers." Isabel said. "GO!"

Ohhhhh! He's NOT making fun of my frog slippers! He LIKES them?!!!

I walked back to the stage. AGAIN. Way nervous. AGAIN. In my frog slippers ...

AGAIN!

But this time ... no screechy microphone! Just CARTER MCLAIN!!!! And me onstage!!!!!!

He held out his hand.

I TOUCHED CARTER MCLAIN'S HAND!!!

"Likin' the frog slippers," Carter McLain said.

And I said ...

GLAK.

(OK! OK! I know Glak? I said GLAK?!!! But tell me what you think YOU'D say if #3 on your Ultimate Crush List is going to sing a song to you?!!!)

And whew! Because nobody heard me say Glak! Because the gajillion Princess girls in the audience were screaming!

AHHHHHHHHHHHHH!

So Carter started singing.

Tonight you are my princess!

He was singing it right to me, me, me!

He was looking at me!

I was looking at him!

OK, and then I heard one girl talking. And it was Sierra.

"Piper, I guess we should've worn frog slippers!"

chapter 15

This Journal Belongs to:

★ Maddy Elizabeth Sparks

Private! Keep Out!!!

Carter McLain sang a song to me!!! And Carter McLain touched my hand!!! The very hand that is holding this pen!

OK, I am still FREAKING OUT. That was the BEST!

And now the 4 A's are having their awesome time! They're off on a limo ride. After they left we all started changing. Into our pajamas.

I'm already changed. So I'm just hanging out.

In my best frog slippers ever!!!! And guess what?

This pajama party isn't even done! Lauren said there's STILL more to come!!!

K! Everyone's here in their pjs! g2g!!!

"I love your pajamas!" Claire told me.

I liked hers, too. Everyone was in their fave pajamas!

Kacey wore a blue t-shirt with princess piggies!

Claire's were white silky long-sleeve shirt and pants.

Isabel was wearing a t-shirt and cargo pj pants.

And mine were pink with puppies wearing princess crowns!

And now everyone was wearing slippers!

We went back into the main room. There were some long tables set up.

An ice cream sundae bar!!!

"Ready for some ice cream?" Lauren asked us. We were like, yeah!!! We got in line. We were all talking with some of the other girls.

Then it was my turn to make my sundae. OK, this was Maddy's Super Special Sundae! Mint chocolate chip with:

- ☆ Hot fudge syrup
- ☆ Crumbled up chocolate cookie pieces
- ☆ Whipped cream

"What did you get?" I asked Kacey. She was eating chocolate chip cookie dough with:

- ☆ Marshmallow sauce
- ☆ Butterscotch syrup
- ☆ Whipped cream

Claire got strawberry with:

- ☆ Strawberry syrup
- ☆ Rainbow sprinkles
- ☆ Whipped cream

Isabel got vanilla with:

- ☆ Caramel sauce
- ☆ Nuts
- ☆ Whipped cream

"OK, I think something major just happened," I announced.

They were all like ... what?

"We all got whipped cream!!!"

"And, so ... huh?" Kacey said, eating her sundae.

"We never get anything the same!" I said. "We like different EVERYTHING tonight! Hairstyles, lip gloss flavors, candy ... I mean EVERYTHING!!"

"You're right," Isabel said. "Totally different."

"But still totally friends," Claire said.

Awwwwww ...

We ate our sundaes. We were talking to some more girls.

"We're back!"

It was the 4 A's! All these girls surrounded them! Asking them a bajillion questions. "What was it like? What was Carter McLain like?"

"The limo was sooo totally fancy!" Ami said. "Way awesome!"

"And of course ... I mean ... CARTER MCLAIN!" Amber shrieked.

"AHHHHH!"

"He was soooo nice!" Allison said. "He even told us some behind the scenes stuff. From this new movie coming out!"

We were all like, EEEEEEEEHHHHHHH!

"This is so the best night of my life," Allison said.

We were all so YAY! for her.

"You guys are sooo lucky," Claire said.

Lauren announced the planned activities were done. And it was time to start getting ready for bed.

But not to sleep!

At least, not this early, hee!

We all put our sleeping bags out all over the floor. Our pillows! Our stuffed animals!

I lay my sleeping bag down. I hoped someone would put theirs next to mine! I hate when it's all stressful! Like when Haley says I want to sleep next to Brittany and then Brittany goes and I want to sleep next to Amanda and then nobody says they want to sleep next to Maddy and I feel really stupid.

Anyway.

Here? I put my blue bag on the floor. And Kacey put her red and black one next to mine! And Claire put her light purple one on my other side! And Isabel put her camo one kinda near the bottom of mine. And yay! We were all together!!!

And right near us? The 4 A's!

I laid out my sleeping bag all nice. I laid down. Comfy. Well, the floor was a little hard. But still. I spread out. Ahhh ....

Then OUCH! Kacey stepped on my hand!

"Oh, sorry, Maddy!" Kacey said.

"The hand!" I said, laughing. "Don't harm the special hand!"

Then I asked for the gazillionth time. "Anyone want to see the hand? The hand CARTER MCLAIN touched?"

"Ack! Enough!" everyone groaned. They'd seen the hand!

I held up my left hand.

"Anyone? Anyone?" I teased.

"Enough of the hand!" everyone moaned. But we were all cracking up!

And then ...

THWAP!

I got thwapped! By a pillow!

"Hey!" I said. I looked around.

Isabel was looking all innocent. Aha!

I grabbed my pillow and threw it back it her.

OOF!

"HEY!" Isabel said.

"You started it!" I said.

"Actually, I didn't," Isabel was laughing.

"Kacey!" I said. I grabbed her pillow off her bag. And ...

WAP!

I whapped her with her pillow!

"Hey!" Kacey said. "It SO wasn't me!"

So we all looked at ...

CLAIRE???!!!!

"Uh oh!" she said. Totally laughing.

And then ... THWAP! THWAP! THWAP!

We all threw our pillows at her.

But one missed! And hit Amber of the 4 A's!

"You guys are gonna get it!" she yelled. And then screamed,

PILLOW FIGHT!!!!!!!!!

AHHHHHHHHHHHH!

THWAP! THWAP! WAP!

Pillows were flying everywhere! Everyone was yelling all ...

HEY!!!!!!!!!!!!! AHHHHHHHH! OOOOOOOOF!

I bopped Kacey over the head! Oof! Isabel bonked me in the stomach! I fell down! But I threw the pillow back at Claire! Wap! She went down!

Everyone was CRACKING UP!!!!

"Attention, girls!"

It was Lauren! Over the microphone! Uh oh. Were we in t-r-o-u-b-l-e?!!

chapter 16

Everyone was totally silent.

But Lauren was smiling. And then Lauren picked up a pillow and then ...

WOP!

She threw it at some girl! And then ...

MORE PILLOW FIGHT!!!!!!!!!!!!!!!!!

WOOOOO HOOOOOOOOOOOOO!!!!!

Wapping! Bapping! Thwapping!

WHEW! I was way exhausted! And laughing! I couldn't breathe!

"Alright, girls," Lauren said. "It's time to settle down. We're turning the lights down."

Everyone settled. Flopped back on their sleeping bags.

"Claire, your stuffed animal is way cute," I told her.

"This is Mr. Cubbles," she said, holding up a cow.

"This is Pommy," I showed everyone my kitty.

"I brought Sebastian," Isabel had a black bear.

"And this is SSSS the snake," Kacey said. She had a green and pink snake. Cute!

The lights got dim.

Then Lauren came walking over. With four girls and their sleeping bags.

"There's a spot over here," she said, pointing to an empty space. "How about this one?"

The four girls started spreading out their bags. Blugh. Piper and Sierra. And their two friends.

"Oh. It's you," Piper said when she noticed me. "YOU'RE over here."

"If you don't like it, feel free to move to another area," Isabel said cheerfully.

"We can't move anymore," Sierra said. "Piper already asked to move twice."

"Well, the air conditioner was cold," Piper said. "And the other spot? Too out of the way."

"Nobody could see us," Sierra whined.

"If she's here to be seen, isn't it a little dark?" Kacey whispered to me, giggling.

"Let's play truth or dare," Piper said.

Her friends were like yeah! Truth or dare!

The rest of us sitting around were like, um, maybe, could be fun.

"It was my idea so I'll ask the questions," Piper said. "Maddy, who's your secret crush?"

Uh, WHAT? My face turned bright red!

"We're all just getting to know each other," Claire said politely. "I think we should ask questions with nicer manners."

"Lame," Piper announced. She turned to someone else. "But OK. Girl in the purple pajamas, what's the stupidest thing you've ever done? Besides wear those pajamas. HA! Just kidding!"

"Hey, isn't that the girl who said mean things to you before?" I heard Ami ask Allison. I remembered! Allison was crying before. I guess it was because of Piper.

ARGH. Piper is so NASTY!

"Pass," the purple pajama girl was saying. "I guess I'll take a dare."

"OK, here's your dare," Piper said. "You have to eat dog food."

Everyone was like, WHAT??? Groooooooooossss!

"This is out of control!" Kacey whispered to me.

"Maybe we should say something to Lauren," Claire whispered.

And then all of a sudden Isabel gave this little scream like "OH!!!"

Everyone was like, WHAT?!!

"I think I heard something," Isabel said.

Everyone was quiet.

"I think it must be, you know," she said. "The Maniac of the Mall."

"What are you talking about?" Sierra said.

"Don't you guys know about the ghost that haunts this mall? I mean, it was in all the newspapers," Isabel said.

"Hey, what about Truth or Dare?" Piper whined.

"Sh!" her friend Brandi shushed her. "What maniac?"

Isabel kept talking. She told about this ghost with one arm. He makes this sound like this: **mooooooooooooooooan!**

All of a sudden the lights got darker!

I felt all shivery.

Isabel said the ghost wants to find a wife to haunt the mall with him. He floats around and someday he's going to grab a girl ... and make her his wife.

And then all of a sudden we heard this noise.

Mooooooan.

"Oh no," Isabel said. "I think I summoned him by talking about him!"

And I looked up. Ohmigoshohmigosh!

There was a glowing white thing! Coming our way! And it grabbed Kacey and ...

ACCKKKKKKKKK!

Everyone screamed!!!!!!!!

And then the lights went up!

And we saw Claire! With a flashlight shining on her white flowy pajamas!

It was CLAIRE!

"Ohmigosh," Kacey said. "I can't believe you did that to me! My heart is pounding like crazy!"

"That freaked me out," Amber said. Everyone was cracking up.

"That was excellent," I said.

"We planned that on the ride over," Isabel said. She high-fived Claire.

"That was weak!" Piper announced.

"Then why did you scream?" her friend Traci said really loud.

HE HE.

"Sierra, you can come out now," Piper said. Sierra was hiding in her sleeping bag!

Everyone was starting to get quiet. Then we saw girls falling asleep. I lay down. I picked up Pommy. We were all whispering. I heard Allison ask Isabel advice about dealing with her parent's divorce.

"That's gotta be hard," I said.

"Yes, family changes are hard," agreed Claire. "Like Kacey's family having a baby."

Then I heard a noise. Like, Sniff! It was Kacey!

"What's the matter?" I asked.

"OK, this is totally babyish," Kacey said. "But I'm homesick!"

Ohhhhh!

Um ... what could I say?

"It's not babyish, some of my friends totally get like that, too!" I said.

"I know it's way late," Claire said. "But if you want, I have some free minutes on my cell phone!"

"OK, thanks!!" Kacey said, all happy. "My Mom won't mind!"

She took Claire's phone and dialed it.

I looked around. People were totally sleeping all over the place. A couple people were snoring.

Heh!

"Pssst, you guys awake?" Isabel whispered. She and the 4 A's came over and sat with us. Then Lauren came over.

"How are you doing?" she asked us. "Did you enjoy yourselves?"

"We had the BEST time," Allison said. "This was soooo fun."

"Is Kacey OK," Lauren asked. "I see she's on the phone?"

"Homesick," I said.

"Well, the other chaperones and I will be over there all night," Lauren said. "If she needs anything, let us know."

Lauren left.

Kacey hung up the phone. She was all smiley again!!!

And then all of a sudden someone got out of their sleeping bag. And started walking over to us.

"Oh no!" said Allison. "That's that girl who was so mean to

me."

PIPER! She was heading our way.

"Well don't worry, if she starts in again ..." Amber looked all tough.

Piper walked over to us and said ...

"Carter?"

We were all like ... HUH?

"Um, what?" Kacey asked Piper.

"Carter, you're so sweet!" Piper said.

"What is she talking about?" I asked.

"Ohmigosh," Isabel said. "Look! Her eyes are closed!"

PIPER WAS ASLEEP! Totally sleepwalking!

And sleeptalking! About ... Carter McLain!

We started to giggle. Then we were all CRACKING UP! I mean, how funny is THAT!!!

And then the craziest thing happened. Piper's eyes opened a

teeny bit. Then she bent over. And she picked up one of my frog slippers.

Then she hugged the slipper.

"Oh, Carter," she said.

She was still totally asleep!

Ohmigosh. This is way too funny. We totally LOST IT.

"Too funny," Kacey gasped. "Can't breathe!"

OK, I have to do this.

I grabbed our sticker camera. And just when I was about to take a picture ...

Piper went like this.

"You're the best boyfriend ever, Carter." And then ...

PIPER KISSED MY FROG SLIPPER!!!!!!

We all went ...

EEEEEEEEEEEEEEEEEeeeeeeeeeeeeeeee!

And ...

CLICK!

I got a picture!!!!

This Journal Belongs to:

Maddy Elizabeth Sparks

Private! Keep Out!!!

OK! My stomach hurts!!! From laughing!! Because ... Piper sleepwalking? Kissing my frog slipper? OK that was the FUNNIEST THING EVER!!!

Isabel walked Piper back to her sleeping bag. Piper laid down. And then we heard this noise: SNORE! SNORE!

Piper was snoring! Way loud!

SECOND FUNNIEST THING EVER!!!

So I showed everyone the sticker photo! Piper smooching my frog slipper! We were like what should we do with it! Make copies and show everyone we knew? Put it on the Internet?

Noooo ... too mean. Piper might be that mean! But we aren't! So here's what I did. I gave it to Allison. And Allison went over and stuck it to Piper's pillow. So Piper is gonna wake up and be all Huh? WHAT IS THIS???!!

Hee.

Yawn. OK. Sleepy. g2g ...

ZZZZZZZZZZZZZZZZZZZZ

chapter 17

"Good morning!" Lauren said. It was morning!

The sleepover was over. Everyone had changed into clothes. Ate bagels and doughnuts. And gone home. I got the e-mail address for the 4 A's. We were sad to say bye! They were sooo nice!

But the TOO Crew was still here! Lauren asked us to stay a couple minutes. We all sat down in a circle.

"The event was very successful," Lauren said. "The girls seemed to have a good time."

We were all like Yeah!

I mean ... Makeovers! Meeting the 4 A's! Focus grouping! Scavenger hunt! Dancing! Ice cream sundaes! Pillow fights! Carter McLain! Ghost stories! Sleepwalkers!

(And Piper's face? When she saw that sticker? She was like HUH???? Totally confused. We all just pretended we were like la la la. No idea why she looks like that. Hee.)

It was soooo fun! Soooo funny!

I rate it a ... **10++++++++**

"Well girls, having fun is most important," Lauren said. "And it was nice we also got a lot of great information from the focus groups."

"It was so funny," I told Lauren. "I mean, me and Kacey and Isabel and Claire? We all liked different things! Lip gloss, candy, t-shirts ... practically everything!"

"You girls certainly are different in many ways," Lauren agreed. "And you know what? That's what makes you such a special team. And on that note ..."

She took out four boxes.

"I'd like to give you girls a thank you present for your help," Lauren said. "And you'll see each one of them is unique, just like you are!"

Oh! Is that what I think it is ...?

I opened it. YES! A charm! A new charm for my TOO Crew charm bracelet! It was a princess crown!!!

Mine had shiny blue jewels sparkling on it!! Kacey's had purple sparkly jewels! Isabel's had orange ones! And Claire's had pink ones!

Our fave colors!!!

Soooo pretty!

We all fastened our new charms on our charm bracelets. They looked so pretty.

"And that's not all," Lauren said. "I have your next assignment. We're going on a trip. The TOO Crew's next stop? New York City."

WE'RE GOING TO NEW YORK CITY!!!!!!!!

I've never been to New York City!

Way glam. Way exciting. Way cool!

We were all jumping up and down! Like 4 Kaceys!!!

"What are we going to do in New York?" Isabel asked Lauren.

"Some fashion. And also, well," she smiled. "I think I have someone else who can explain it well. Be right back."

She got up and went out the door.

We waited.

"Doesn't my charm bracelet look beautiful?" I asked. I held up my hand. "Especially on my left hand?"

"Oh no," Isabel groaned. "Do we have to see the hand again?! Not the hand!"

"Yes," I teased. "THE hand that THE Carter McLain touched. See it?" I got up and stuck my hand next to Isabel. She was cracking up.

"See?" I held it up to Kacey.

"I see the hand!" she laughed.

"Claire," I said. "Do you know that Carter McLain touched this very hand? The Cutie Pie #3 on my Ultimate Crush List that is CARTER MCLAIN!"

And then all of a sudden everyone went, "OH!"

And then I heard a voice.

"May I see The Hand?"

A guy's voice. Um ... I turned around. There was Lauren. And ...

CARTER MCLAIN!!!

Red-face Rating: ☆★☆☆☆ out of ☆★☆☆★ stars.
Because Carter McLain just heard every word I just said.

And everyone cracked up. Including Carter McLain!

"Oook, I think I'm done with The Hand," I said. I sat down really quick.

Ohmigosh.

"Anyway, I thought it would be fun if Carter would tell you about your next trip," Lauren said.

"We're going to have a movie premiere for my next movie," Carter said. "The one where I play a prince."

A movie premiere? Like you see on TV! Wayyyyy glam. And then get this:

"I'd like to invite the TOO Crew and some chaperones to attend," Carter said.

The TOO Crew meaning us? We get to go to a movie premiere?!

"We'll need a little help from you on the trip," Lauren said. "And then we'll celebrate your hard work with the movie premiere. How does that sound?"

How does that sound? A movie premiere? In New York City?

AHHHHHHHHHHHHHHHHHH!!!

That sounds AMAZING!!!!!!!!

We were all jumping all over the place!

I high-fived Kacey! Then Isabel! Then Claire!

I looked at Kacey! And Isabel! And Claire! We were going on another trip! Together! We were all so different! But together we made an awesome TOO Crew! And awesome friends!!!!!!

Happy Face Rating:

 out of

the end ... but just for now!

See you in New York City! Stay TUNED!

OK bye! This is the end! But not 4ever of course!
Because remember ...

We're going to New York City next!!! WOW. That is so
major. Just wait til you see what awesome, exciting
things are going to happen. It's going to be totally cool!!!!

So get ready for Tuned In Episode #8 coming exclusively
to Limited TOO!

Luv ya!
♡

Maddy ♡

P.S. OK! I have way exciting news. I can hardly even believe it myself. But it's true. Announcing the ...

TOO CREW's NEW MINI-SITE!!!

YES! If you go to LimitedToo.com there is a new area for girls like you called, "Messages from Maddy and the TOO Crew!"

TOO Crew Things to Do you can't find anywhere else!!

And exclusive sneak previews for upcoming Tuned In Books!!

And INSIDE SCOOP about the books!!!!!

You have to check it out!!!!! New on LimitedToo.com!!!!!